MARJORIE
WEINMAN
SHARMAT

What Are We Going to Do About Andrew?

PICTURES BY RAY CRUZ

Aladdin Books
Macmillan Publishing Company
New York

Collier Macmillan Publishers
London

Aladdin Books
Macmillan Publishing Company
866 Third Avenue, New York, NY 10022
Collier Macmillan Canada, Inc.

First Aladdin Books edition 1988

Printed in United States of America

10   9   8   7   6   5   4   3   2   1

Library of Congress Cataloging-in-Publication Data

Sharmat, Marjorie Weinman.
What are we going to do about Andrew?

Summary: Andrew's abilities to fly and to turn
himself into a hippopotamus confuse his family until
they come to terms with his exceptional powers.
[1. Family problems—Fiction]   I. Cruz, Ray, ill.
II. Title
[PZ7.S5299Wh   1988]   [E]   88-3357
ISBN 0-689-71264-2

For Andrew Richard Sharmat,
of course —M.W.S.

To B.K. from R.C.

"What are we going to do about Andrew?" asked Andrew's mother as she and Andrew's father were sitting on their front porch watching Andrew fly by. "He's the only boy on the block who flies."

"I know," said Father. "Still, there may be other flying boys in this world. We only know about this block."

"Well, it certainly makes me nervous to see him up there flapping his arms and legs and swooping all over the place," said Mother.

"Watch the clouds instead of Andrew," said Father.

"I try," said Mother. "But Andrew rather spoils the view."

The next day Andrew and his brother Figaro went to school.

"Andrew," said the teacher, "please name and describe a large animal."

"I can do more than that," said Andrew. And he turned into a hippopotamus.

by KARINA

102

When Andrew and Figaro got home from school, Figaro said, "Andrew turned into a hippopotamus in school today."

"What happened then?" asked Father.

"The teacher gave Andrew an A," said Figaro.

"What do you have to say about that, Andrew?" asked Father.

"I was the only one in the class to get an A," said Andrew.

"Andrew is a good student," said Mother.

The next day Andrew said, "Philomena asked me to play with her all day."

"I'm glad you have a good friend like that," said Father.

After Andrew left, his mother said, "Not everyone wants a friend who flies and turns into a hippopotamus."

"Philomena is a true friend," said Father.

Andrew's mother and father went outside to weed their garden.

"Today smells so fresh and fragrant," said Mother, "that I know everything will be all right."

"You mean with Andrew," said Father.

"That's what I mean," said Mother. And she pinned a violet in her hair.

Andrew went to Philomena's house.

"Let's play hide-and-seek," said Andrew. "You be *it*."

"Okay," said Philomena. She covered her eyes.

Andrew flew to a roof and hid behind a chimney.

"I heard you take off!" cried Philomena. "No fair flying!"

Philomena ran from the yard. "I'm telling," she said.

She ran to Andrew's mother and father.

"Andrew and I were playing hide-and-seek and Andrew cheated. He flew," said Philomena.

"Oh dear," said Andrew's mother. "Just when today was smelling so sweet."

"There's Andrew now," said his father, looking up. "Andrew, come down here this instant."

Andrew landed between his mother and father.

"Now, Andrew," said his father, "your mother and I have noticed that you've been flying around for the last month or so. But we didn't say anything to you because, after all, it's up to you how you spend your free time. And if you want to change into a hippopotamus now and then, that's up to you, too. But *not playing fair*. That's something else again. You know very well that Philomena can't fly, so when you play hide-and-seek with her, you *must* stay on the ground. Is that clear?"

"It's clear," said Andrew. He turned to Philomena. "I'm sorry," he said. "I'll play fair."

"Okay," said Philomena. "Let's start again."

Andrew's mother and father continued to weed their garden.

Suddenly his mother sat down on the bed of tulips.

"Look where you're sitting," said Father.

"Oh dear," said Mother. "I was thinking about our problem instead of the tulips."

"Our problem?" said Father.

"Yes, you know we have a problem," said Mother. "We have a son who flies. Now I *do* like to encourage Andrew in whatever he does and he does fly beautifully."

"Yes, he has a perfectly executed swoop," said Father.

"But what must people think?" said Mother. "He's not even playing a proper game of hide-and-seek."

"That's not all," said Father. "It's that hippopotamus thing, too. What do I pack for his lunch when he goes off to school in the morning? Suppose he changes into a hippo at lunchtime? A sliced cheese sandwich and a Thermos of milk might not be nearly enough."

Father sat down beside Mother.

"Poor tulips," said Mother.

When Andrew came home, he found his mother and father sitting on the tulips.

"What's the matter?" asked Andrew.

"Well," said Mother, "it's about your flying and turning into a hippopotamus. Your father and I are certainly pleased that you can do these things. But there are problems."

"Problems?" said Andrew.

"Yes," said Father. "We do realize that a hippopotamus is a perfectly fine animal. . . ."

"It's a *lovely* animal," said Mother. "But you see, Andrew, neither your father nor I are hippos. Not even part-time. So having a hippopotamus for a son, even occasionally, well it *is* difficult."

"Oh," said Andrew.

He sat down on the tulips.

"And about your flying," said Father. "We've never had anybody in our family who could do that. Your brother Figaro leaps quite well, but that's about it. We've always had our feet on the ground. *Not flying* has been, well, a family tradition."

Andrew lowered his head. "I like flying and I like turning into a hippopotamus."

Suddenly Andrew stood up. "I've got to think about this," he said.

"Fine. Think," said his mother.

"Absolutely," said his father.

Andrew flapped his arms and took off.

"Not up there!" cried his mother.

But Andrew was already flying high over houses and treetops.

In a minute he was out of sight.

"I hope he comes back soon," said Father.

Andrew's mother and father sat and waited.

"No sign of him," said Father, looking at the sky.

"No sign of him," said Mother, looking in the garden.

They waited and waited.

But Andrew did not return.

"Maybe he'll come back tomorrow when everything looks sunny and cheerful," said Mother.

The next day Andrew's mother and father went out and sat on the tulips. But there was still no sign of Andrew.

"He must be having an extremely long think," said Mother.

A week passed. Now everyone on the block was worried about Andrew.

"Such a fine, polite boy," said one of the neighbors. "He always waved when he flew by."

"Always," said another neighbor. "Perhaps he went south for the winter."

Philomena was crying. "Maybe he turned into a hippopotamus near a zoo or a circus," she said.

"Andrew is far too clever to do that," said Father.

"Andrew is the only hippopotamus ever to get an A," said Figaro.

"I hope that wherever he is, he's eating three good meals a day and going to bed on time," said Mother.

"Don't worry," said Father. "Andrew is very trustworthy."

"Yes, Andrew is trustworthy and clever and polite," said Mother.

"And he is a kind and loving son," said Father. "He always raked the leaves before the yard got messy and he lets us sleep late on Sundays."

"And he was full of such wonderful surprises," said Mother.

"Every day was exciting because of Andrew," said Father.

"I certainly miss his flying by," said Mother.

"And I miss his turning into a hippopotamus," said Figaro.

"There is so much to miss about Andrew," said Father.

"Andrew is a wonderful boy," said Mother. "But now he's gone."

"No, I'm not," said Andrew. "I was up there think-ing. I sat on a mountaintop. I flew around steeples. I visited a wild animal farm. But all I could think about was how much I missed you."

Andrew kissed his mother and father.

"I brought you a daffodil and some cheesecake," he said.

"Your father and I are very lucky to have you," said Andrew's mother.

That night in the middle of dinner Andrew turned into a hippopotamus.

Father gave Andrew three helpings of everything.

"I'm so pleased that Andrew has such a good appetite," said Mother.